This edition published by Parragon Inc. in 2013

Parragon Inc.
440 Park Avenue South, 13th Floor
New York, NY 10016
www.parragon.com

Written by Peter Bently
Illustrated by Emma Foster and Deborah Melmon
Edited by Laura Baker
Designed by Rachael Fisher and Jo Russell
Production by Jonathan Wakeham
All photos courtesy of iStockphoto

ISBN 978-1-4723-2001-8

Printed in China

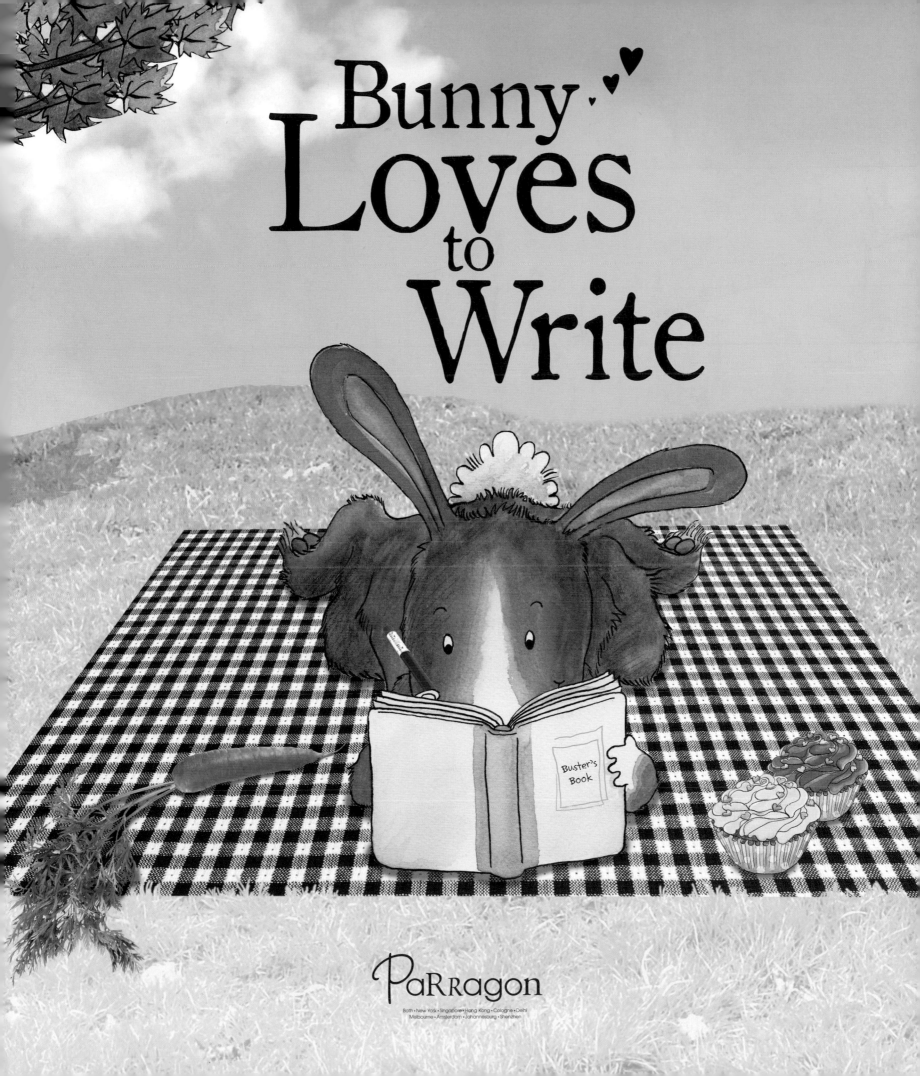

# Bunny Loves to Write

## PaRragon

Bath • New York • Singapore • Hong Kong • Cologne • Delhi
Melbourne • Amsterdam • Johannesburg • Shenzhen

One day, Buster was going out to play.
"Always carrying a book!" chuckled Mom. "What is it this time, Buster? An adventure? A ghost story?"

"It's not a storybook," smiled Buster. "It's a notebook. My teacher wants everyone in the class to make up a story." "That sounds fun," said Mom. "What are you going to write?"

"I don't know," said Buster. "I can't think of anything!" "Oh, you'll have lots of ideas soon," said Mom. "But write them down right away or you'll forget them!"

Buster started walking to the park. Soon he met his friend Francine.

"Mom packed us a picnic," she said. "Lend me a paw with this heavy basket!"

"A picnic? It feels more like treasure!" grunted Buster.

Then he took out his notebook. "I've just had my first idea! My story could be about treasure!"

They kept walking toward the park, but soon Francine stopped.

"I'm sure I just saw Max," she said.

"Me too," said Buster, puzzled. "But it looks like he's disappeared!"

"As if by magic!" smiled Francine.

"Magic, huh?" said Buster.
"Maybe someone could do magic in
my story. Like a wizard!"

Suddenly ...

**BOO!**

Max jumped out from behind a bush.
"Eek! You scared me!" laughed Francine.

"And you've given me another idea," said Buster. "Something scary! There could be spooky ghosts in my story!"

The three friends started crossing a stream near their friend Sam's house, when—

Buster's Book

SPLASH!

"Phew!" grinned Buster. "At least my notebook didn't get wet! And I've just had another idea. One of the characters could live in water."

"Like a mermaid," suggested Max.
"Or a frog!" said Francine.

"Hi, everyone," said Sam.
"I'll be ready in a minute.
Do you want to come up and
wait?"

Sam's
Place

"What, up there?" gasped Francine.
"No way! You're almost in the sky!"

"Now there's an idea," said Buster. "There could be planes in my story."

"Or space rockets," said Max. "Or aliens!" said Francine.

When they got to the park, the friends met Bella, Buster's sister.

"Hi, everyone!" she said. "Hey, Buster, what are you writing?"

"I'm writing a story," said
Buster. "I've had lots of ideas,
and now I'm making them into
a real adventure!"

"Cool," said Bella.
"Can we hear it?"
"Okay …" said Buster.
"But it isn't finished yet."
Buster opened his notebook
and began to read.

One day, Gus and Ella found a chest in the attic. It was so heavy!

They opened the lid.
The chest was
full of gold!

"Thank you!" said the wizard.
"You found the lost
treasure of Meowlin!"

But the very next night,
the treasure vanished.

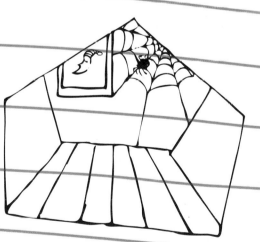

Where had it gone?

So the wizard waved his wand, and they all flew to Mars by magic!

"That's as far as I got," sighed Buster. "I told you it wasn't finished yet."

"We'll finish it for you!" cried Sam.

"Cool!" said Buster. "You can all write a little bit each."

Everyone took turns writing in Buster's notebook.

"Okay," he said when they were finished. "Here's the rest of the story!"

Fantastic, thanks, everyone! There's just one last thing to add.

And he wrote:

Gus, Ella, Fiona, and the wizard all lived happily ever after.

THE END

"Hooray!" said Francine. "But the story isn't quite finished."

"It isn't?" said Buster. "What happens next?"

"Easy," laughed Francine. "They all eat the treasure!"